The Wonderful World of Murali and Hridya

(Children's literature - Educational Fiction)

By

P. Anil Prasad

Title:
The Wonderful World of
Murali and Hridya
(Children's literature - Educational Fiction)

Author:
P. Anil Prasad

Published year: November 2025
Publisher: Author
ISBN: 978-93-5592-343-1 (Paperback/ softback)

Printed on demand at Kindle Direct Publishing (KDP)

Thanks to Google Gemini and Grok Imagine for illustration images

Reader age: *Ideal for children aged 7 to 14 years, the stories in this book help them develop essential life skills, including communication, empathy, socialization, reasoning, problem-solving, organization, emotional intelligence, and responsibility. More volumes containing stories on the above theme will follow. Parents and teachers also encouraged to read and share it with their children / students for educational purposes.*

Author's Note

Dear little friends,

Do you know what makes our lives bright and happy? It's starting to learn and play when we are very small! Good Early Childhood Care and Education (ECCE) is like planting a strong seed that grows into a big, beautiful tree. It helps us become curious, kind, brave, and smart. It builds the best foundation for our whole life and makes the world a better place for everyone!

This book is a small gift to help make that dream come true.

Come, let's go on a fun adventure! Meet Murali, Hridya, and their loving family and friends. They laugh, play, learn new things, and spread joy everywhere they go. There are wonders, surprises, and little challenges that they solve with curiosity, courage, intelligence, and kindness.

I believe you will love reading about them!

Dear parents, grandparents, and teachers—are you ready to read this story with your dear little ones?

With love,
Anil

November 20th 2025

Acknowledgement

I'm truly thankful to all who helped me to understand the needs of education and training, and enriched it through shared discoveries.

A big thank you to my bosses and colleagues who made me a part of key projects like the Additional Skill Acquisition Programme (ASAP) under the Higher Education Department, Government of Kerala, India, delivering skill training to thousands of school and college students.

To the thousands of students and learners I've interacted with since I started teaching at the age of fifteen: your questions, curiosity, and insights made learning a truly fun, two-way experience. Thank you!

Above all, my lifelong gratitude goes to Dr. K.M. Abraham, former Chief Secretary to the Government of Kerala and CEO of ASAP Kerala. He guided me like an elder brother—with unwavering care, profound wisdom, and countless opportunities that shaped my path.

I'm also deeply grateful to the Commonwealth of Learning (COL), Canada, for the valuable international opportunities that broadened my understanding of open education and global learning systems.

Dedication

To all my wonderful little friends all over the world!

Table of Contents

1. Hridya the Smiling Doll

From the moment Hridya was born, she stole the show in her family. She was adorable and always so cheerful. Right from her first day, she woke up with a big, bright smile. Her big brother, Murali, nicknamed her "the smiling doll."

Murali was seven when Hridya arrived. Ever since Mom told him a new baby was on the way, he couldn't wait. When she finally came, his happiness exploded. It was a cozy evening at the hospital in town. Murali waited with his Dad, Mahadevan, his grandparents, and everyone else outside the delivery room, where his Mom, Madhurima, was. After what felt like forever, a nurse popped out grinning. "A baby girl... you've got a little sister!" she told Murali. They named her Hridya.

Three days later, Mom and the baby came home. Murali and his grandparents spruced up the place to welcome them. Dad was there too, helping out. The whole house buzzed with joy, like everything was brand new and sparkling. Murali thought, "Wow, a baby makes home feel magical!"

Murali made it his mission to look after Hridya. He loved every second. She slept peacefully most of the time and only whimpered softly when hungry. One day, Mom, while she was feeding Hridya, teased Murali, "When you were this tiny, you'd wail super loud if hungry and get all fussy if we were slow." She laughed. Hridya paused and stared at Murali. He turned red, wondering if she understood.

Every time felt like his first babysitting adventure. He watched Hridya with tons of love and wonder. Her sleepy faces and wiggly moves when awake were the cutest. He got really good at reading her signals. Sometimes she reached for toys; other times she wanted to scoot closer to things. He knew when she just wanted Mom, or playtime, or food, or a trip outside. It made caring for her easy. In weeks, he mastered the basics of babysitting. His parents, grandparents, relatives, and friends all cheered him on. But the best part was Hridya loving his care—that meant the world to him.

Dad, Mahadevan, and Mom, Madhurima, were teachers. Grandparents also lived with them, like best buddies. The family was tight-knit, full of love and respect. Murali picked up babysitting tips from all of them.

Another set of cool teachers was Grandpa's walking crew. Grandpa rose early for his 5:15 a.m. morning walk. Murali didn't want him to go alone, so he woke up at 5 and tagged along. He loved the quiet, fresh mornings. Grandpa pointed out some neat natural phenomena, such as how the air cools, how mist forms, clues about rain, and why plants are essential. There were always fresh chats.

As they walked, Grandpa's friends joined in, making the experience even more enjoyable. They treated Murali like their own grandkid. From their talks, he learned that being a big brother was a huge responsibility. "I have duties just like Mom, Dad, and my grandparents," he thought proudly. He loved that.

Auntie Manjula, one of Grandpa's friends and a pediatrician, was like a grandmother. She visited their home often and shared facts about baby growth. Once, Murali asked her, "When will Hridya chat and walk with me?" She chuckled and said, "By her first birthday, she'll say 'mama' and 'papa,' wave 'bye,' and understand 'no.' She'll stuff things in cups, hunt for hidden toys, stand, and cruise along furniture. Some kids start walking alone early. Hridya will zoom ahead, I bet."

"How do you know?"

"Watching kids closely teaches us," she said with a smile.

Murali couldn't wait to see it. He helped Hridya with everything. She lit up around him. He stuck close when she was awake. Even while doing schoolwork, he played with balls and rattles with her.

During his morning walks with Grandpa and his friends, Murali learned that when a new sibling comes, share the spotlight happily. Let parents focus more on the baby. "Am I doing that?" he wondered at that moment.

Months flew by, and Hridya started calling for Murali with wiggles and special sounds. Parents took time to catch on, but Murali got it instantly. Their bond was that strong already.

***

Life-Skills Introduced in This Chapter

Adaptability to Change: *Welcoming a new family member, like a baby sibling, and adjusting to the excitement and shifts in family dynamics with joy and patience.*

Observation and Empathy: *Learning to read a baby's signals (such as hunger, play needs, or desire for closeness) to provide caring support and build a strong bond.*

Responsibility in Caregiving: *Taking on babysitting duties, mastering basics like watching over a sibling, and seeking guidance from family and experts to improve skills.*

Learning from Others: *Gaining knowledge about child development and sibling roles through conversations with parents, grandparents, and knowledgeable adults, such as a pediatrician.*

Sharing Attention: *Understanding the importance of letting parents focus on the new baby while happily sharing the family spotlight to maintain harmony.*

2. Hridya's first steps

Once babies hit nine months, everyone starts buzzing about when they'll walk on their own. When Hridya turned nine months, Grandpa told Murali, "Hey, kid, you took your first steps at nine months and two weeks. I bet Hridya does the same." That got Murali excited because he had been daydreaming about strolling hand in hand with his little sister. She was already saying "Papa" and "Mama," just as Auntie Manjula had predicted. She'd even made up the word "Tattu" for Murali. When folks asked her name, she'd chirp "Pittu." Soon, "Tattu" and "Pittu" became fun nicknames around the family and friends.

It was a lazy Saturday afternoon. After lunch, Hridya and Murali plopped on a mat in the living room, playing away. Hridya did not eat much yet, but loved joining the table like a boss, getting served all the goodies just like the grown-ups.

Mom and Dad were at school because it was a workday for them. Grandma relaxed by the window, flipping through the newspaper. Grandpa tinkered in the garden out front. Mid-play, Murali rolled a soft ball to the corner. Hridya zoomed after it on all fours, snagged it, and giggled like she had won a prize, showing it off to Murali.

"Come on, sweetie, bring it back!" he cheered.

Out of nowhere, Hridya popped up, stood tall, and dashed right to him. Murali froze, jaw dropped. Only when she crashed into him with the ball did he snap back, hugging her tight. "Grandma... Hridya just walked!" he yelled, pumped up. Grandma had seen it too, her eyes wide. She peeked out the window and called to Grandpa, "Hey there... Hridya walked!"

Grandpa dashed in, thrilled. Hridya tried again, heading for Grandma, but spotted Grandpa and switched directions, running to him. He scooped her up, planted kisses on her cheeks, and beamed, "Great job, my little star!"

Grandma and Murali clapped like crazy. When Grandpa set her down, she bolted back to her favorite brother.

The house exploded with joy, and even at school, Mom and Dad's coworkers buzzed about it. Grandma called Mom, who was in the staff room during a free period. Mom shared the news with her friends there, itching to tell Dad when his class ended. Everyone asked for sweets to celebrate, so Mom and Dad promised some the next day.

Murali burst with pride now that she could walk. His dreams took a leap forward, picturing walks to school together. The next day, he shared the news with Grandpa's walking buddies. They swapped fun tales of the first steps their siblings, kids, and grandkids took. Each story packed helpful facts and tips for him.

***

Life-Skills Introduced in This Chapter

Patience and Anticipation: *Waiting excitedly for important milestones, like a baby's first steps, while understanding that everyone develops at their own pace.*

Encouragement and Support: *Cheering on family members during play and new challenges to help them build confidence and try new things.*

Celebrating Achievements: *Recognizing and joyfully marking small victories, like a first step, with hugs, claps, and shared excitement to strengthen family bonds.*

Sharing Joy with Others: *Spreading happy news with family, friends, and community, and using celebrations (like sweets) to include everyone in the moment.*

Learning from Stories: *Listening to others' experiences and tales to gain tips and insights about growth and family life.*

3. A brotherly senior student

Murali always knew that being a big brother was a big deal, full of essential duties. And he absolutely loved it.

Having Hridya in his life changed him in wonderful ways. He began to see the little kids at school as if they were his own siblings. He was always ready to help them out. His school had a pre-primary section for the youngest kids and a primary section for the older ones, separated by a vast playground. Each group had its own play areas, but sometimes the bigger kids—especially the boys—would sneak into the tiny tots' spot. Murali used to join in occasionally, but now he understood how scary that could be for the small ones. They might trip or get bumped. So, he stopped and even told his buddies to do the same.

The start of the school year was always exciting for the older kids. They loved watching the new pre-primary students. Some little ones cried a lot, others tried to fight back tears, and a few even bolted away. But there were always some who smiled brightly. The big kids would whisper, "What's that kid so happy about?" Now, Murali couldn't stand seeing the tears or hearing any mean comments. His heart ached for the little ones. If it were Hridya, he knew he'd feel heartbroken. At the bus stop, he let the small kids board first and helped them climb on safely.

In those early months, the new pre-primary kids often wandered into the wrong classes. Teachers and helpers kept an eye on them during arrivals, breaks, and playtime. Still, sometimes the tots ended up in the primary section by mistake. Before heading to his own class, Murali would scan the area to spot any lost little ones and gently guide them back to where they belonged. Yes, he was turning into a super responsible senior with the caring heart of a big brother.

There was another spark that made Murali so thoughtful. He never forgot Grandma's tale about Chirag. Chirag grew up with farmer parents in a small town in Karnataka, India. They worked as gardeners for the local park and became exceptionally skilled at it, earning numerous compliments. When Chirag was three, his parents pursued better jobs in larger cities across different states. Chirag tagged along, switching schools five times before high school. At first, it was tough, but he quickly learned to fit in.

Chirag was especially friendly to the younger kids. In ninth grade at a new school, he spotted a seventh grader named George, who had physical challenges but was super bright. Chirag helped him whenever he could, and they became close friends.

One day, George asked Chirag, "You're so kind to everyone. How do you stay that way?"

Chirag grinned and said, "This is my fifth school, George. Teachers, students, and folks helped me through all the moves, besides my parents. Without them, I would never have made it this far. I figure the best way to say thanks is by being kind and helpful to others around me."

Those words stuck with George forever. He grew up to be a renowned surgeon, always available to help those in need, day or night. It made him known worldwide. George never forgot Chirag's support and told everyone it was Chirag's wisdom that shaped him. He always quoted Chirag: "The only way to keep saying thanks to those who helped me is by staying kind and helpful to folks around me."

***

Life-Skills Introduced in This Chapter

Empathy and Compassion: *Recognizing how younger children might feel scared or lost and responding with kindness, like helping them at school or on the bus.*

Responsibility as a Role Model: *Taking on duties as an older sibling or senior student, such as guiding lost kids and discouraging unsafe play to protect others.*

Paying It Forward: *Learning from stories of kindness (like Chirag's) to show gratitude by helping others, creating a cycle of support and goodwill.*

Observation and Awareness: *Scanning surroundings to notice when someone needs support, such as spotting wandering toddlers, and acting thoughtfully in response.*

Self-Reflection and Growth: *Changing personal habits (e.g., stopping sneaky play) based on understanding others' perspectives, inspired by family stories and experiences.*

4. The magic of being together

Murali's parents left home early each morning for school, taking their breakfast and lunch with them. Murali ate his breakfast by 7 a.m., just before heading to his own school. At that time, Hridya was still fast asleep. His grandparents ate later, after helping Hridya with her morning routines and feeding her. The only days the whole family could eat together were holidays. But even then, Murali was busy babysitting Hridya, playing with friends, doing homework, or reading books. When his parents and grandparents called him to join them for meals, he always said, "Don't wait for me!" He usually showed up late, when they were almost done or had already finished. They often reminded him how important it was to eat together, but he didn't take it seriously.

One day, during a morning walk, an interesting debate popped up among Grandpa's friends. The topic was the various types of teams people join throughout their lifetime. It started with the question: "What is the first team in anyone's life?" Grandpa's closest friend, Uncle Ahmed, said without a doubt, "Definitely, it's the family. No question about it." Murali's grandpa agreed, adding, "True, a mother and child form the very first team—not just for people, but for all living beings."

After a short discussion, everyone nodded in agreement.

"You know, the biggest strength of any team is knowing each other well and being ready to help one another. You'll find that in all successful teams," Uncle Ahmed continued.

"Yes, and it's the key to a happy family too," someone added.

"For that to happen, everyone—even the busiest person—should make time for family," another friend suggested.

"Absolutely! We all need to sit together, talk, and support each other. Eating together is especially important, I'd say," yet another person commented.

"I remember a story my grandma used to tell me when I was little," Auntie Manjula from the group began.

As usual, the story had a king. This king had three sons and three daughters. He was a wise and beloved ruler, admired by everyone in the kingdom. But the king was worried. His children quarrelled all the time and didn't seem to love one another. Noticing the king's concern, the Raja Guru—the king's chief advisor—asked what was wrong. The king explained about the fights among his children. The guru had witnessed it many times and had been waiting for the right moment to discuss it. Now was the time. He asked the king, "How often do you spend time with your whole family?"

"Only on special occasions," the king replied. "I know it's important, but you understand how busy a king's days can be."

"Your Majesty, your family is your closest kingdom," the guru said. "You should get support and inspiration from them first. To do that, you need to spend time together."

"But how?" the king asked.

"I suggest you all eat together," the guru proposed. "Sharing meals can create a lot of positive energy. It's proven! Let me review the daily schedules of you, the queen, the princes, and the princesses. I'll find a way for everyone to meet at the table twice a day."

"You have my permission," the king said right away.

The guru planned for the royal family to gather in the dining room for meals twice a day. At first, the princes and princesses even quarrelled at the table. However, as they continued to meet and sit together, the fights became less intense and occurred less frequently. Soon, they started serving food to one another and speaking with love and respect. They learned about each other's favorite foods and discovered their likes and dislikes in other things as well. Gradually, they began to understand and accept their differences. It brought magical changes to the royal family's home, making the king very happy. He praised the guru and offered him gifts. But the wise guru politely refused, saying, "Your Majesty, the greatest gift for me is your happiness. It's a gift for the entire kingdom!"

"That's the magic of eating together," Auntie Manjula finished. "My grandma always ended the story that way, and she made sure our family did it too."

Murali loved the new idea of "family time." Now he understood why his parents and grandparents kept encouraging him to eat with them. From that day forward, he made it a priority.

***

Life-Skills Introduced in This Chapter

Prioritizing Family Time: *Making an effort to spend quality time with family, even when busy, to build stronger relationships and support.*

Eating Together as a Bonding Activity: *Recognizing how sharing meals can reduce conflicts, increase understanding, and create positive energy in a family.*

Listening to Elders' Advice: *Paying attention to guidance from parents, grandparents, and wise adults to learn valuable lessons about teamwork and harmony.*

Understanding Teamwork in Family: *Viewing family as the first "team" in life, where knowing each other well and helping one another leads to happiness and success.*

Accommodating Differences: *Learning to respect siblings' likes, dislikes, and differences through regular interactions, leading to fewer quarrels and more love.*

5. Let Your Sibling Know You Love Them

It was a bright Sunday afternoon. Though the days were hot, a comfortable coolness filled their house, thanks to the big shade tree in the courtyard and a cluster of banana plants on the other side. Their home was situated in a quiet neighborhood with plenty of trees, a nearby lake, and a gentle stream flowing from it—all of which helped keep things cool and pleasant.

Murali was helping his little sister Hridya play with a new set of toys their parents had bought her the day before. Hridya was almost three years old and loved her toys dearly. Suddenly, the doorbell rang, and Murali's mother opened the door. It was Nadira, Murali's classmate, who lived just down the street.

Murali's mother welcomed her warmly. "Come in, sweetie!"

"Is Murali here, Auntie?" Nadira asked.

"Yes, he is! He's showing his sister how to play with her new toys. Have you had lunch?"

"Yes, thank you, Auntie." By then, Murali had come into the living room and greeted her. "Hey, Nadira!"

"Okay, kids, you three can play together now," Murali's mother said. "I need to finish preparing for next week's classes." With that, she headed to the study room.

Murali and Nadira joined Hridya, who was playing, and sat on either side of her. "Look, Hridya, who's come to see you!" Murali said. Hridya looked up from her toys, saw Nadira, and smiled sweetly. Even though she'd only met Nadira a couple of times before, she remembered her right away. Nadira gave her a gentle kiss, full of love and joy.

"How do you get to have this little queen by your side all the time, Murali?" Nadira asked, hugging Hridya. "My brother is about the same age, but he hardly ever comes near me. He cries if I get too close to him. I'm so jealous!"

"It's pretty easy, Nadira," Murali replied with a laugh. "I just stay close to Hridya all the time, so she doesn't have to come looking for me."

"Oh, come on! That's not some big secret. I try to be with my brother too, but he doesn't like it. That's the problem."

"Sometimes Hridya also gets lost in her own little world and doesn't look at me or respond. But if I start to move away, she cries right away."

"What does that mean?"

"Babies want their loved ones nearby, even when they're busy playing or exploring. Once you understand that, they'll want to stay close to you, things become easy."

"But I'm sure my brother doesn't like me being around."

"Hmm... have you ever shouted at him?"

"Yes, a few times—when he messes up my things, like my books."

"Ah, I see the issue. Kids get scared and pull away from people who shout at them."

"Then how do we teach them not to spoil important things?"

"We do need to guide them, but in a gentle way."

"How?"

"At this age, they understand a simple 'No' when you say it kindly to stop them from doing something. If they pause or stop, give them a hug or kiss to show you're proud. They get that too. Remember, don't explain too much—they won't understand long talks. Just say a caring 'No,' like 'No, my good boy...' and see how they react."

"Have you tried that with Hridya?"

"Yes, lots of times! Especially when she tries to grab sharp things like pens or pencils. It works great."

"That's cool! Give me more tips on how you talk to Hridya."

"Sure. One thing Hridya loves is when I help her finish words she's trying to say."

"For example?"

"Kids learn words like 'Mom' or 'Dad' quickly. At first, when she sees Mom coming, she'd just say 'Mmm...' I'd know she meant 'Mom,' so I'd say, 'Yes, Mom! Mom is coming!' She'd smile so big, like she was saying, 'You got it!'"

Both Murali and Nadira laughed, and Hridya, not understanding why, joined in with her own sweet giggle.

"Any more tips?"

"Little kids love toys that make sounds, like rattles. Help them shake them and make noise—it's fun! You can also point to things they like and name them in a sing-song voice. For example, point to a bird or a flower or a ball and say, 'Look at that... It's a flower!' or 'Look at that... It's your ball!' Singing it like a rhyme makes them enjoy it more."

"You're like an expert! Tell me more."

"You can teach them other important things the same way."

"Like what?"

"For example, when you're washing your brother's face, sing softly as, 'Hey, my boy, I'm washing your face...' Do it over and over, and he'll start to understand both the action and the words."

"How did you learn all this?"

"Remember I told you I go on morning walks with my grandpa and his friends?"

"Yes!"

"From my Grandma, Mom and there's a pediatrician in the group, Auntie Manjula. I learned these from them."

"Thanks, Murali! I'm eager to try this at home. I really want my brother to know I love him. Do you think it'll work?"

"Absolutely, Nadira."

They spent the rest of the afternoon playing with Hridya, trying out Murali's tips. To Nadira's delight, they worked! In the evening, full of confidence and happiness, Nadira headed home.

***

Life-Skills Introduced in This Chapter

Empathy and Presence: *Understanding that young children need the comforting presence of loved ones nearby, even when they're absorbed in their own activities, to build trust and closeness.*

Gentle Discipline: *Using a calm, caring 'No' instead of shouting to guide behavior, and following up with positive reinforcement like hugs or kisses to encourage good responses without fear.*

Effective Communication with Toddlers: *Helping young children complete words they're trying to say, which boosts their language skills and makes them feel understood and supported.*

Engaging Play: *Encouraging play with sound-making toys and pointing out/naming objects in a fun, sing-song manner to stimulate curiosity, learning, and bonding.*

Teaching Through Routine: *Incorporating simple songs or rhymes into everyday activities (like washing) to help children learn actions, words, and self-care enjoyably.*

6. A Conflict Resolved

Years passed happily, filled with fun events. Murali was now a ninth-grade student, and Hridya had started third grade. Their schools shared the same large campus.

Every year, Murali's school celebrated its annual day in the first week of November. Hridya's school held theirs in the last week of November. Auditions for that year's events were coming up soon. Murali and his eight friends wanted to perform a group item in the fest. Hridya cheered her brother —she couldn't wait to see him on stage. Every evening on the rattling school bus, Hridya pressed her shoulder to his and whispered, "What will you do?"

"Anything," he said, "as long as it's excellent."

She nodded, solemn as a judge.

One rainy afternoon, during a free period, Murali and his friends gathered in the school auditorium to decide on their item. Rain was drumming on the tin roof like impatient fingers. Ideas ricocheted: drama, dance, mime, magic, stand-up. Voices rose, then tangled. They knew time was running out to start practicing for the audition.

"Why can't we do a drama?" one asked.

"What's wrong with a group dance?" another said.

"Is mime a bad idea?" a third wondered.

The suggestions and debates continued for a long time.

Their physical education teacher, who overheard them from afar, walked over.

"Haven't you picked anything yet? Will you decide before the end of the year?" Though he teased them at first, he quickly turned serious. "Well, kids... There are six of you... Okay... what's the first thing to think about when choosing a stage performance?"

Jonson, mud on his knees from morning practice, answered, “What are we all good at?”

“Exactly. So?”

Silence. Rain. When no answer came right away, the Teacher said, "If you're a team of good friends, it should be easy."

"Yes, sir, we are good friends," they all chimed in together.

"Then tell me your choice," the Teacher said with a smile.

They huddled again, foreheads almost touching. Minutes later they straightened.

“Mime,” they said in one breath.

"Great choice! How did you decide so quickly now?" the Teacher asked.

"Sir, you gave us the hint," Jonson explained. "As a team, we know each other's strengths and weaknesses. We’ve been miming each other for years,” Jonson grinned. “Invisible walls, fake rain, the works.”

“I’ve noticed,” the teacher said. “Even during assembly prayers.” – All laughed.

The friends got excited and dashed out into the rain. The Teacher called after them with a grin, "Hey, I won't encourage that!" But as he turned away, his own grin betrayed him—he could still taste rain on a college rooftop. His smile grew brighter.

On the bus ride home that day, Murali told Hridya they had chosen Mime. He explained what Mime was and how they'd perform it. Murali sketched invisible boxes in the air for Hridya. Her eyes widened; she traced the edges with him. “Teach me tonight,” she demanded.

“Deal,” he said, and meant it.

***

Life-Skills Introduced in This Chapter

Team Decision-Making: *Discussing ideas openly in a group to reach a consensus, even when everyone has different opinions, to avoid wasting time.*

Identifying Strengths: *Recognizing shared talents and abilities within a team to choose activities that play to everyone's strengths.*

Seeking and Applying Advice: *Listening to guidance from teachers or mentors to resolve confusion and make better choices.*

Resolving Conflicts: *Turning debates into productive talks by focusing on common ground, reducing arguments through understanding.*

Sharing and Teaching Skills: *Enthusiastically passing on what you've learned to siblings or others, like teaching Mime, to build bonds and encourage growth.*

7. A Kind Offer to Help

It was a cold December morning. Murali and his grandpa went out for their usual morning walk. The mist was thick that day, making it hard to see anything beyond thirty meters. However, the wide path, lined with streetlights, guided them safely. Others joined them at their regular spots along the way. Someone in the group said, "We should thank the local authorities for keeping this path safe and comfortable for everyone, especially us older folks." Everyone in the walking group wore sneakers, warm sweaters, gloves, and woolen hats.

Murali slowed down to walk beside Uncle Damodar. Lately, he'd noticed Uncle Damodar struggling to keep up with the group's normal pace. Uncle Damodar was about eighty years old and a businessman. After padding for a bit, Murali asked, "Uncle, are you having any trouble?"

"Yes, my boy," Uncle replied. "My left knee has been bad for a long time. Now it's really painful. The doctor says I need surgery."

"Then why haven't you done it yet?"

"I have to, child. But someone needs to stay with me in the hospital for a few days. After that, I'll need help for a couple of weeks too. Your aunt isn't well, as you might know." He paused, then added, "I could hire help, but your aunt would feel happier and more comfortable if our son were here. So, I'm waiting for him to take leave."

"When will your son come?"

"He's working on an important project at his company right now, so he can't take time off. He might come in four months."

"Oh, that's a long wait! Don't worry, Uncle. My school closes next week for winter vacation. Please schedule your surgery then. I'll stay with you." Hearing this, the old man's eyes filled with tears. He gently patted Murali on the shoulder with love and said, "I'd be so happy to have you there, my son. But it might be tough for you. I can wait four or six months—it's not a big deal."

Murali called out to his grandpa, who was a few steps ahead. "Grandpa, did you know about Uncle Damodar's knee problem?" Grandpa stopped, turned around, and said, "Yes, he's had it for a while, and he's planning surgery." The others stopped too and listened.

"But Uncle's plan is taking too long," Murali explained. He shared their conversation and repeated his offer to stay at the hospital.

"You have a wonderful heart, dear Murali. I'm so proud of you," Grandpa said. "You enjoy your holidays. I'll stay with him." This sparked a friendly competition in the group—everyone wanted to help Uncle Damodar. Finally, they decided to take turns, one at a time. The group praised Murali for his kindness and willingness to lend a hand. Uncle Damodar planned to visit the hospital that day to see the doctor and schedule a surgery date.

***

Life-Skills Introduced in This Chapter

Empathy and Observation: *Noticing when someone is struggling, like an elderly person walking slowly, and asking kindly about their well-being to offer support.*

Offering Help Voluntarily: *Stepping up to assist others in need, such as volunteering time during vacation to care for a friend or neighbor during illness or surgery.*

Community Cooperation: *Encouraging group involvement to solve problems, such as taking turns to provide care, fosters a sense of teamwork and shared responsibility.*

Respect for Elders: *Showing care and patience toward older adults by listening to their concerns and prioritizing their comfort and health.*

Initiative and Problem-Solving: *Identifying delays in someone's plans (like waiting for family) and suggesting practical solutions to make things happen sooner.*

8. Love What You Learn

It was lunchtime at school. The chatter of students from everywhere echoed off the colorful walls of the classroom, adorned with posters of historical figures and science diagrams. After eating, Murali settled in his seat and carefully sketched diagrams of plant cells. His pencil scratched softly as he labeled chloroplasts and mitochondria, preparing for the first period after lunch. Then his friend Saurabh bounded over, his school uniform slightly rumpled from a quick game of football in the playground, a bead of sweat still on his forehead. Standing in front of Murali with a grin, Saurabh peered at the chart and asked:

"Murali, how do you always score full marks in biology? I can't even imagine it! Last test, I barely scraped a pass."

"Why not, buddy? Biology is a fascinating and easy subject," Murali replied.

"I don't think so," Saurabh said, slumping his shoulders dramatically, his voice laced with frustration.

"Why?"

"There's just so much to study! Diagrams, processes, Latin names—it's overwhelming."

"All subjects have a lot to learn," Murali countered gently, gesturing toward the courtyard outside. "But in biology, you can see most of what you study right around you in real life. Take photosynthesis, for example... just look at those plants out there! The way the sunlight hits the leaves, turning carbon dioxide and water into food—it's happening right now, keeping the whole tree alive and growing. Imagine if we could do that!"

Saurabh leaned closer to the window, his eyes widened as he watched a butterfly flutter from one flowering hibiscus to another in the garden outside. "Huh, I guess you're right. But how do I make it stick in my head?"

"Let me ask you something," Murali continued, his tone warm and enthusiastic, like a big brother sharing a secret.

"What?" Saurabh asked curiously, turning back with a spark of interest.

"How many relatives do you know by name?"

"Probably more than fifty—uncles, aunts, cousins from both sides of the family."

"How do you remember all those names without mixing them up?"

"Because I see them often at weddings and festivals, or hear stories about them during family dinners. Plus, I love them. How could I forget Uncle Raj who always brings sweets, or Aunt Priya who tells the best jokes?"

"That's my point, buddy!" Murali exclaimed, clapping Saurabh lightly on the back "You see them, talk about them, and care about them deeply. Just do the same with your studies. Build that connection."

"What do you mean exactly?" Saurabh tilted his head, genuinely intrigued now.

"Observe all the living things around you—those plants in the courtyard, the stray dogs playing near the gate, even your own body breathing and moving. Like them, learn about them with curiosity, and think about how that knowledge can help you and others in the future. Want to be a doctor someday? Understanding cells could save lives. Or a farmer? Knowing soil microbes could grow better crops. Approach it that way, and biology becomes simple, fun, and something you actually look forward to."

Saurabh nodded slowly, a thoughtful smile creeping onto his face as he glanced again at the vibrant garden, where students' laughter mingled with the rustle of leaves. "Hmm... that sounds like a smart idea. I'll try it—starting with watching the ants marching in a line by the kitchen back at home. See if it works for me." Both of them laughed.

"It will, I'm sure," Murali said confidently, giving his friend a fist bump that assured mutual support. Just then, the school bell rang sharply from the tower, its metallic chime cutting through their classroom, signaling the start of afternoon classes.

***

Life-Skills Introduced in This Chapter

Relating Learning to Real Life: *Connecting school subjects like biology to everyday observations—such as plants in the school courtyard or insects during breaks—to make studying more engaging, memorable, and grounded in the world around us.*

Developing a Positive Attitude Toward Learning: *Viewing subjects as interesting and useful by focusing on their practical value, like linking biology to future careers or daily wonders, and fostering a genuine love for the topic through personal relevance.*

Memory Through Connection and Affection: *Remembering information more effectively by forming emotional ties and associations, much like recalling family names through love, frequent interactions, and shared stories.*

Encouraging Peers: *Sharing helpful study tips with friends in a supportive, enthusiastic way—through smiles, gestures like fist bumps, and relatable examples—to motivate them, strengthen friendships, and create a collaborative learning environment.*

Curiosity and Experimentation: *Trying new approaches to learning, such as actively observing nature in familiar surroundings like the school garden or playground, to discover what works best personally and spark ongoing exploration.*

9. Amina's Idea

Amina and Murali were best friends in tenth-grade C division, the kind of duo who turned boring lunch breaks into biology debates. Both were obsessed with living things—how plants breathed, how insects tricked predators, how a single seed could outsmart a drought. So when their biology teacher announced a field trip to the city's famous botanical garden, they practically vibrated with excitement.

Tuesday, 8 a.m., August heat already sticky. The school bus rumbled eighty kilometers north with windows rattling. Two hours later they spilled out into a sea of school uniforms, camera-clicking tourists, and the sweet, peppery smell of crushed marigolds underfoot. It was a crowded day there.

"We might not enjoy this much," a disappointed Murali said to Amina. She stared at the crowd without replying right away. Finally, their teacher got entry tickets for everyone, and they went inside. The crowd was even thicker there.

The garden exploded with color and sound. A giant banyan tree stretched its aerial roots like green waterfalls. Orchids the size of dinner plates clung to bark, glowing neon pink and lemon yellow. Butterflies stitched the air in loops of sapphire and gold. A pond glittered with lily pads big enough to sit on, and koi fish flashed like living coins beneath. Somewhere, a peacock screamed, half laugh, half trumpet.

But the paths were a stampede. Kids darted between legs. Tourists blocked signs to snap selfies. Someone's ice-cream cone splattered across Murali's shoe.

"How can we see things properly in this mess?" Murali worried aloud to Amina. She agreed that a bit more order was needed. She was watching a line of ants marching single-file along a railing, unbothered by the chaos. An idea sparked.

"Hey," she said, "what if we became the ants?"

Murali raised an eyebrow. "Explain, genius."

"Discipline spreads, right? Like pollen on wind. If we move in one calm line—shoulder to shoulder, no shoving—others might copy us. Especially the other schools."

"I'm not sure anyone will pay attention to us."

"Let's try, my friend."

"Okay, let's talk to our teacher."

They shared Amina's idea with the Teacher, who got excited and called it excellent. The message spread quickly among the students. Within minutes, C division formed a perfect column: two-by-two, hands behind backs, chins up like mini soldiers. They marched. At first, elbows jabbed. A tourist's backpack clipped Amina's ponytail. Then—

A fifth-grader from another school peeked over. "Cool! Can we join?"

Soon, three schools linked up. Then five. The line snaked past the cactus dome, where spiky giants stood like green porcupines, and the medicinal herb patch that smelled of mint and mystery. Each group paused exactly two minutes at every sign. Then tourists, amazed, fell in behind the students. The whole garden started flowing like a river instead of a riot.

At lunchtime, they sat in a circle around a large shade tree, where eating was allowed, and shared the food they'd brought. While munching, the Teacher and classmates praised Amina for her brilliant idea. Amina felt inspired by the kind words. They stayed exploring until evening.

On the bus ride back to school, Murali told Amina, "You're a real genius!"

"I should thank you for that," Amina replied.

"For what?" Murali asked.

"I could only share the idea with our Teacher because you supported me. Thanks, buddy!"

***

Life-Skills Introduced in This Chapter

Creative Problem-Solving: *Coming up with practical ideas, like forming a disciplined group, to handle chaotic situations effectively.*

Leading by Example: *Demonstrating good behavior, such as staying organized in a crowd, to inspire others to follow and create positive change.*

Teamwork and Collaboration: *Discussing ideas with friends and teachers, then working together as a group to implement them successfully.*

Persistence in Trying New Approaches: *Willing to test an idea even when doubtful, to see if it can improve a challenging experience.*

Gratitude and Mutual Support: *Appreciating friends' encouragement and expressing gratitude for their unwavering support, which strengthens relationships.*

10. Fear of strangers over a summer camp

Murali's school was organizing a three-day summer camp after the final exams. Fifty students from eight nearby schools would join, with fifteen from Murali's school as the hosts. Only ninth- and tenth-graders were eligible to participate. Students had to apply voluntarily, and teachers would select the final group.

In Class 9C, the buzz was electric. Boys swapped rumors of midnight treasure hunts; girls traded playlists for the campfire sing-along. Only one desk stayed quiet. Lyla sat with her elbows on the scarred wooden surface, tracing the grain with a fingertip, her dark braid slipping over one shoulder like a question mark.

Lyla was a studious, quiet girl who mostly talked to just a few friends, including Murali. Seeing her lack of interest, Murali asked, " Lyla, you're not applying?"

"No." The word came out flat, final.

He leaned closer, voice dropping to the conspiratorial hush they used during group projects. "Come on. Three days of no homework, no uniforms, just games and ghost stories."

She glanced up, eyes the color of rain on concrete. "Ghost stories with fifty people I don't know? Pass."

Murali waited. He'd learned that with Lyla, silence was an invitation, not a wall.

"It's not the games," she said finally. "It's the... noise. The eyes. Everyone sizing each other up like we're in some reality show audition." She hugged her arms. "I get tongue-tied. My brain freezes, and I stand there like a statue while the moment slips away."

He nodded, remembering the time she'd frozen during the inter-house debate, cheeks flaming as the microphone squealed feedback. "Remember when we had to present that science project on volcanoes? You thought you'd combust."

"I did combust. Inside."

"But you didn't. You spoke. And the volcano erupted baking soda all over Physics teacher's shoes." He grinned. "Legendary."

Murali thought for a moment, unsure what to say. Then he asked, "Don't you go to family events?"

"Yes."

"But there are strangers there too—like at a wedding of a family friend. You might meet people you've never seen before." Lyla stayed quiet. Murali added, "At the camp, at least fifteen kids will be from our school, plus our teachers will be there to help."

"I know, but I can't spend three whole days with people I don't know well. What would I even say to them?"

"If that's the worry, let me share something cool. One of the uncles from my morning walk group once said, 'You can handle any new group with simple words like "hello," "how are you," "your face looks familiar," or "have we met before?" And chat a bit about the weather.' I think you should join the camp and try it!"

"That's interesting, but I'm not sure I can do it that easily." She still sounded doubtful.

"How will you know if you don't try?" Murali encouraged her. He pulled a crumpled camp flyer from his pocket, smoothing it on the desk. The paper smelled faintly of the photocopier—hot plastic and ink. "Look, fifteen of us are hosts. We'll be your buffer zone. And the teachers? They're bringing that old bus with the busted air-conditioning. We'll be too busy fanning ourselves to judge anyone."

Lyla traced the camp logo—a cartoon tent under stars. "What if I say something stupid? Like, 'Nice weather' when it's pouring?"

"Then you laugh. Or you blame the monsoon."

She snorted. "Right. What if they ask about hobbies and I blank?"

"Tell them you collect silences. Very rare." Both of them laughed at that.

"Will you be going? If you are, maybe I'll try."

"I'm super excited for it! Promise me you'll apply too."

"Okay... I'll try." She said it with a small smile. Murali knew that was her way of saying 'yes'. Lyla's fear of strangers began to fade, and she felt more at ease with the idea. Sharing her worry with Murali had given her more confidence to face it.

***

Life-Skills Introduced in This Chapter

Overcoming Shyness: *Building courage to interact with new people by recognizing that initial strangeness can disappear through simple conversations.*

Using Conversation Starters: *Learning basic phrases like "hello" or comments on the weather to ease into talks with strangers and make social situations less intimidating.*

Encouraging Others: *Supporting friends by listening to their concerns and offering positive advice to help them try new experiences.*

Trying New Things: *Understanding that you can't judge your abilities without giving something a shot, like joining a camp to grow socially.*

Sharing Problems for Support: *Opening up about fears with trusted friends to gain confidence and perspective on handling challenges.*

11. Apologize First

Murali's family was planning a big party at home for Hridya's seventh birthday. They invited about fifty close relatives and friends to join them in celebration.

The day before her birthday, everyone was busy getting ready for their little princess. Murali had his tasks too—some from his mom, others from his dad. Right after breakfast, Dad asked Murali to wash all the plant pots in their small garden. There were two dozen of them. As Murali got ready to start, Mom asked him to go to the nearby store for a few things. She handed him a list and some money. He agreed.

Meanwhile, his parents went out for shopping other things. Murali thought, "There's plenty of time. I'll clean the pots first, then go to the store."

He began washing the pots, but it took longer than expected, and he forgot about the store. He even skipped lunch to finish. Just as he wrapped up, his parents came home. Mom headed straight to the kitchen and looked for the items she'd asked for. Not finding them, she called Murali. "Where did you put the things from the store?"

That's when he remembered. "Mom, I didn't have time to buy them," he said simply.

"Where did your time go? I asked you this morning. Are you getting lazier as you grow up?" Mom sounded angry.

Murali had worked hard all day, even without lunch, so her words stung. "How can I do everything when you both give me so many tasks at once?" he replied, a bit upset.

"If you were as responsible as you say, you'd have finished both by now," Mom teased. That made him even madder. "I'm not going to the store!" Tears started rolling down his cheeks. He ran to the side yard where no one could see him cry.

Grandma had overheard everything. She saw Murali rush off, then went to the kitchen. "Don't upset him more," she told her daughter. "The poor boy hasn't eaten lunch yet. I'll get him to go to the store after he eats."

"Hmm," Mom replied.

After a few minutes, Grandma found Murali in the yard. "You did a great job cleaning those pots, son. Aren't you hungry? Wash up and come eat. I haven't had lunch either, since you were working so hard."

She kissed his forehead, which calmed him down. "Grandma, I didn't mean to forget. Cleaning the pots was tougher than I thought."

"I know, dear. Want a tip for handling things like this next time?"

"What is it?" Murali asked, wiping his tears.

"There are two sides here. First, you worked hard and finished what Dad asked— that's wonderful! Second, you forgot Mom's task along the way."

"Yes, but it wasn't on purpose."

"I know it wasn't. Still, it's a small mistake. If you'd said sorry for forgetting first, then explained why, Mom would have understood right away. See what I mean?"

"Hmm..." Murali thought about it.

"Now, wash up quick. Let's eat lunch together, then go to the store. Deal?"

"You're coming too?"

"Yes, my dear."

"Okay, Grandma—that's great!" Murali cheered up. He knew she'd probably buy his favorite treats too.

***

Life-Skills Introduced in This Chapter

Taking Responsibility for Mistakes: *Acknowledging when you've forgotten or overlooked a task, even if unintentional, to maintain trust and harmony.*

Apologizing First: *Starting with a sincere apology before explaining reasons, to de-escalate conflicts and show respect in family interactions.*

Managing Multiple Tasks: *Prioritizing and balancing chores or duties, while learning from oversights to improve time management.*

Handling Emotions Calmly: *Dealing with frustration or anger by stepping away to cool down, and accepting comforting advice from elders.*

Seeking and Applying Guidance: *Listening to wise tips from family members, like grandparents, to resolve issues and grow personally.*

12. The Success Secrets of Uncle Pavithran

One bright January morning, Uncle Pavithran joined Murali and Grandpa's daily walking group. He was the newest member of the neighbourhood and had only recently retired. Before that, he had led the human resources department of a large company, travelling to many countries and major cities across India. Now settled in a house nearby, he accepted Grandpa's warm invitation to walk with the group. Uncle Pavithran was humble, cheerful, and full of gentle humour. Everyone looked forward to hearing his experiences.

One day, Uncle Damodar asked, "How difficult was it to manage so many people?"

"It was never simple," Uncle Pavithran replied with a smile. "My job was to pick the perfect people for the company and help them do things fast, work smart, and stay super happy. Most importantly, I had to glue them together so they worked like one big, strong team. It was tough, yet deeply rewarding."

"Rewarding?" someone wondered aloud.

"Indeed," he continued. "When you break a large challenge into smaller steps and solve them one by one, the process becomes enjoyable. Success follows, and soon you begin to love the challenge itself. This is true for any task—whether at work, school, or home."

Grandpa nodded. "What kept your team so closely connected?"

"They shared both work troubles and personal worries with me," Uncle Pavithran explained. "For job problems, they wanted solutions. For personal matters, they sought advice. That showed trust. People open their hearts only when they feel safe. Trust, therefore, was the bond that held us together."

"You are absolutely right," said Uncle Damodar. "But building strong trust takes time. How did you do it?"

"Trust grows slowly, like money saved in a bank," Uncle Pavithran answered. "Every helpful act, every kind word, every kept promise adds a little 'value' to an invisible account in someone's mind. Over time, that value earns 'interest'—and the interest is trust. The more value you add, the stronger the trust becomes."

"What a clear picture!" exclaimed another walker. "And if someone breaks a promise?"

"Then value is withdrawn," Uncle Pavithran said. "A small mistake takes away a little. A serious breach can empty the account completely—and turn friends into strangers."

Murali listened in silence, his young mind turning over the idea. Who holds an account for me? Do I hold one for others? A quiet conversation began inside his head.

On another morning, someone asked, "Did you solve every problem your team brought to you?"

"No one can solve everything," Uncle Pavithran replied honestly. "But listening with an open heart can lighten the burden greatly. When people share their worries with someone they trust, simply being heard brings relief. Often, that alone solves half the problem."

Grandpa added, "Listening shows respect. It tells the other person, 'Your feelings matter. I understand.'"

Murali thought about his own life—at school with friends, at home with family—and wondered how these lessons might fit.

***

Life Skills Introduced in This Chapter

Building Trust in Relationships: *Earn trust gradually by being helpful, caring, and keeping promises—like adding value to a "mental bank account."*

Active Listening: *Listen with full attention and an open mind. This reduces stress for others and shows respect, even if no solution is needed.*

Enjoying Challenges: *Turn big tasks into small, manageable steps. Celebrate each success until the work itself becomes enjoyable.*

Self-Reflection: *Pause to consider how ideas apply to your own life—such as asking, "Who trusts me? Do I trust them?"*

Learning from Elders: *Pay careful attention when experienced adults share stories. Their wisdom offers valuable guidance for daily life.*

13. Guiding with Courtesy

The science exhibition in February every year at Murali's school was famous, drawing visitors from all around.

The sun shone hot over the school yard. The big science fair turned the whole school into a fun place full of surprises. Under tall trees with red flowers falling like rain, kids set up tables with bubbly volcanoes, tiny cars that run on sun power, and spinning planet models that glow like magic. The air smelled like sour juice from the volcanoes, fresh batteries, and sweet ice pops from the snack uncle under his colorful umbrella. Speakers boomed with news.

Student volunteers usually handled guiding the crowds, with ten captains each leading a team of ten helpers. The physical education teacher oversaw everything. That year, Murali was selected as a captain. The three-day event saw attendance far exceeding expectations, straining both volunteers and staff. In certain sections, tensions escalated into verbal disputes between guides and guests. By contrast, the zones assigned to Murali's team remained orderly and serene, with no incidents of conflict.

At dusk, the courtyard lamps flickered on, casting golden pools across the exhibits. Mrs. Lakshmi, the principal, convened the debrief in the auditorium, aimed at refining operations for the remaining days. Physical Education teacher opened the discussion: "Let us first recognize outstanding performance. Murali's sector recorded zero disputes. The atmosphere was consistently courteous and composed.". A loud applause.

Mrs. Lakshmi, seated on the dais beneath a portrait of the school founder, commended Murali and beckoned him forward "Share your method, Murali".

“There was no secret formula, ma’am,” Murali replied. “We began with a clear objective: to provide every visitor with a positive, stress-free experience. In our initial team meeting, we defined courtesy as the cornerstone of that objective.”

“Excellent,” the principal responded. “How was this implemented?”

“We established a three-phase protocol,” Murali explained: "First, greet each visitor with eye contact, a slight bow, and the phrase, 'Welcome to the World of Wonders', next, accompany guests at their side, speaking calmly regardless of ambient noise, and tailor explanations to their interests and finally conclude the visit with the words, 'Thank you for joining us—please proceed safely to the next exhibit,' along with an open-palm gesture.

Then the physical education teacher inquired about crowd-control measures. Murali continued, “We anticipated high density and rehearsed responses to common irritants—obstructed views, impatient parents, or fatigue. For instance, if a child could not see a demonstration, a team member was trained to offer, ‘May I briefly lift your child for a clearer view?’ We limited such interventions to thirty seconds to maintain flow.”

"How did you develop these ideas and train your team?" - another student captain asked.

"Buddy, we watched training videos on managing crowds and events. Our computer teacher helped us use the lab to find the best ones. Then we practiced what we learned."

The principal requested a brief demonstration of those videos. Ms. Sonia, the computer teacher, projected the selected clips on the auditorium screen. Murali provided concise commentary, illustrating adaptations for the school context. The presentation concluded to sustained applause.

Mrs. Lakshmi directed that all captains adopt the protocol by the following morning and scheduled Murali to conduct early briefings for each team. The subsequent two days witnessed a marked improvement in visitor experience across the exhibition. One parent, initially frustrated on the opening day, returned on the final afternoon to express gratitude and present a token of appreciation.

***

Life-Skills Introduced in This Chapter

Leadership and Goal-Setting: *Leading a team by setting clear goals, like creating a polite experience, and discussing ways to achieve them.*

Preparation and Planning: *Anticipating challenges, such as crowds, and preparing strategies in advance to handle them effectively.*

Learning from Resources: *Using educational tools, like videos, to gain skills in areas like crowd management and applying them through practice.*

Courtesy and Conflict Resolution: *Staying polite to calm upset people and turn potentially noisy situations into positive ones.*

Sharing Knowledge: *Presenting ideas and experiences to others, like explaining training methods, to help the group improve together.*

14. The Right Thing to Do

The large yellow school bus moved steadily along its busy morning route. Soft golden sunlight streamed through the windows, lighting up tiny dust particles floating in the air.

Every day, Murali and his little sister Hridya rode this bus to school together. That morning, Murali sat by the window, holding Hridya close. She placed her butterfly-themed school bag on her lap and sat quietly. After a while, she whispered to him in a worried voice:

"Brother, will you come to my class today and stop some students?"

"Oh, my little one! Stop students? Why, darling?"

"Some classmates always push me from behind when we're playing or lining up. They try to snatch things from my hands and my bag, too."

"That's not nice at all. Who are those classmates?"

Hridya named three students. "Have you asked them nicely not to push or grab your things?" Murali asked.

"Yes, brother, lots of times. Now you must stop them!"

"What if I talk to your teacher about it?"

"But my friend said the best way is to call you to stop them."

Murali laughed softly. "Where did your friend get that idea?"

"She saw it in movies. In movies, big brothers always step in like that."

Murali smiled, kissed her forehead gently, and said, "That's not the right way, dear. Movies aren't like real life or school. I know your Teacher well—she was my teacher too. I'll ask her to take care of it. She'll fix things, I promise."

"Okay, brother. Tell her to stop it right away!"

"I'll see her today."

With the confidence from her brother, Hridya started singing a new rhyme she'd learned in class. Murali smiled, happy to see her anger melt away. He hugged her close and sang along with her. Then they could see their school in the distance.

***

Life-Skills Introduced in This Chapter

Seeking Non-Violent Solutions: *Choosing peaceful ways, like talking to a teacher, over fighting or punching to resolve bullying or conflicts.*

Distinguishing Fiction from Reality: *Understanding that ideas from movies may not work in real life and can lead to wrong choices.*

Asking for Help from Trusted Adults: *Turning to teachers or family for support when facing problems like pushing or grabbing at school.*

Encouraging Open Communication: *Asking others nicely to stop bad behavior first, before escalating the issue.*

Building Confidence in Siblings: *Reassuring younger family members to help them feel safe and turn negative feelings into positive ones.*

15. A great game plan

It was a Wednesday evening; the sky already turned into violet above the school playground. Many students stayed after school on the playground to practice for the upcoming zonal sports meet.

Murali was on the volleyball team—the best in their district. Victory seemed almost inevitable, but the whole squad practiced hard—except Ashraf. He was an amazing middle-blocker, quick at reading opponents' moves. Though he played well, he often looked sad.

During the practice, Murali spiked the ball so cleanly the net barely shivered. The rest of the volleyball squad drilled with hungry focus. Ashraf rose like a blade for every block, yet his landings carried the weight of something heavier in his mind. Murali sensed something was bothering him.

Murali jogged over to Ashraf during the water break, towel around his neck and said: "Buddy, is everything okay? You seem down."

Ashraf wiped his face, buying time. "Oh! It's nothing!"

"That's the exact sentence people use when they're drowning," Murali said, voice low enough that only Ashraf heard. "Come on. I'm listening."

Ashraf glanced at the coach, then at the empty stands. "After practice. Bench by the neem tree." – he said.

An hour later the court was quiet, the ball bags zipped shut. They sat shoulder to shoulder, the wooden bench still warm from the day's sun.

Ashraf spoke first, words small. "Money's tight at home. Always has been. Dad's a daily-wage mason; Mom stitches blouses at home. I'm scared… tenth will be my last exam."

Murali let the silence settle, the way his mother taught him—give sorrow room to breathe. When he finally answered, it was gentle. "I'm really sorry, Ashraf! That fear is real. But quitting school feels like surrendering the one ladder you've already climbed halfway."

"Even if I want to climb, my head's full of bills. How do I listen to teachers when I'm calculating rent?" Asharaf said it by fixing his eyes somewhere far away.

Murali turned to face him. "Remember the semifinal against St. Joseph's? You read their setter's shoulder twitch and blocked three straight points. Same brain, different court. We'll treat every challenge in life like an opponent's serve—watch the pattern, jump early."

Ashraf gave a short, doubtful laugh. "Easy to say."

"Not easy. Doable. These are my plans for you" Murali counted on his fingers. "One: we make the district merit scholarship our match point. My parents have the forms, the deadlines, even sample essays. Two: we study together—library, 4 p.m. sharp. Three: if I snag a scholarship too, the cash is yours. Deal?"

Ashraf stared at the goalpost shadows stretching across the sand. A small flicker crossed his face, the first spark of possibility. "You'd split your prize?"

"Team rule," Murali grinned. "Middle-blockers don't let teammates drop."

Ashraf's shoulders loosened; the knot inside his chest untied one twist at a time. He rubbed his palms together, the way he did before a serve. "Library. 4 p.m tomorrow. I'll bring the Physics textbook."

"And I'll bring samosas," Murali said. "Fuel for future engineers."

They bumped fists. It sounded sharp in the cooling air. As they walked toward the gate, the last of the light slipped behind the neem tree. Dusk arrived gentle and generous while crickets were tuning their evening orchestra. A breeze filled air with the faint sweetness of jasmine from the school garden. Fireflies blinked on like tiny stadium lights, celebrating two boys who had just turned worry into a game plan.

Under that quiet, hopeful glow, Ashraf's steps felt lighter. Tomorrow the court would demand sweat, but tonight the world felt wide enough for a better future.

***

Life-Skills Introduced in This Chapter

Empathy and Active Listening: *Recognizing when a friend is upset and providing a safe space for them to share their concerns without judgment.*

Problem-Solving Creatively: *Brainstorming practical solutions, like aiming for scholarships, and applying skills from one area (sports) to another (studies).*

Encouraging Perseverance: *Motivating others not to give up on goals, such as education, by focusing on achievable steps and building confidence.*

Teamwork and Support: *Offering to study together and share resources, like scholarships, to help a friend overcome challenges.*

Seeking Help from Adults: *Recognizing when to involve trusted grown-ups, like parents or teachers, for advice on important issues like finances or education.*

16. In the Camp; The Opening Day

The summer camp days that Murali and his friends had been eagerly awaiting finally arrived. Nestled in the lush green campus of his school, surrounded by tall coconut palms swaying gently in the warm breeze and vibrant hibiscus flowers blooming along the paths, the camp promised a magical escape from the hot April sun. Fresh mangoes hung from nearby trees, and the distant call of koels added a sweet melody to the air.

Vice Principal Indira, a kind woman with a warm smile and a neatly tied sari, was in charge. Everyone had to report by 5 p.m. on April 10th. By 4:15 p.m., all fifty participants were there, including Lyla, who clutched her small backpack with excitement.

After a quick check-in, they walked to the large meeting hall. The hall was a spacious room with high ceilings and colourful charts on the walls—maps of Kerala, drawings of elephants, and houseboats gliding through the backwaters. Murali, Lyla, and the other thirteen children from their school knew the place well. For the thirty-five students from eight different schools across the state, the wide campus with its shady verandas and sparkling pond felt brand new.

"Look at those butterflies!" whispered a girl from Thrissur, pointing to a cluster of blue ones fluttering among the hibiscus flowers.

At 5:30 p.m., Teacher Indira stepped in and gave her welcome speech.

"Dear children, I'm thrilled to see fifty bright faces! I already know fifteen of you, and the other thirty-five are my new friends. Welcome to camp—you are all like my own children now. I promise this will be a fun adventure for everyone. We'll enjoy nature walks, folk dances under the stars, and even make fresh coconut laddoos together."

A boy from Kozhikode raised his hand politely.

"Ma'am, will we get to play in the pond?" he asked, eyes wide with hope.

Teacher Indira laughed softly. "Yes, Arjun, but only after we learn safe swimming rules from an instructor. Safety first, remember?"

Arjun was amazed—she had remembered his name! He felt at home at once.

Then the teacher turned to Lyla. "And Lyla, I see your sketchbook. What will you draw for us?"

Lyla blushed but answered clearly, "I want to draw campfires and games, ma'am—maybe all of us holding hands."

"Wonderful!" Teacher Indira smiled.

She explained that the camp would have two kinds of activities: some planned by the teachers, like, story circles about Kerala's legends and early-morning yoga, and others created by the children themselves. No teacher would stand over them to check behaviour. They had to show the best manners and self-control on their own.

"Trust yourselves to be kind, helpful, and honest," she said. "That is what makes a true camper."

After the speech, Teacher Indira sent them to the sleeping areas.

"Arrange your space as if it were your own little home—tidy, respectful, and ready for sharing. Be back here at 6:30 p.m."

The dormitories were bright classrooms turned into cosy corners. Low wooden beds wore crisp white sheets;

small bamboo shelves waited for bags. The children moved quietly, following the rules.

Murali unfolded his mat, smoothed every wrinkle, then folded his clothes into neat squares. Water bottle, flashlight, storybook—everything stood in a perfect row. "No clutter here," he whispered, proud.

Beside him, Lyla lined up her hairbrush, soap case, and pencils.

Ravi from Palakkad watched and grinned. "My shelf looks messy—let me fix that!" He straightened his towel and socks with careful hands.

No one rushed or grabbed. They passed things with soft "please" and "thank you," turning tidy-up time into a gentle game. When they finished, every corner shone like a tiny, happy garden.

At 6:30 p.m. sharp, fifty children sat cross-legged in the hall. Teacher Indira's eyes twinkled.

"Welcome back! Your challenge: plan tomorrow from 5 a.m. to 1 p.m. Morning yoga and the rest of the day are already fixed. Include waking up, brushing, breakfast, breaks, and fun events. Write clear goals and steps. Teachers will not help—you are the planners! You have until 9 p.m. We'll discuss for forty-five minutes, then enjoy a late dinner at 10 p.m.—a small change from home routines. Ready?"

"Yes, ma'am!" fifty voices rang out.

Priya from Ernakulam leaned forward. "Ma'am, what if we have different ideas?"

"Speak kindly and vote fairly," Teacher Indira replied. "Listen to every voice—that is how leaders grow."

"Your time starts… now!"

The teachers stepped out. Fifty heads bent together, pencils scratched, and the camp's first adventure began.

***

Life-Skills Introduced in This Chapter

Taking Initiative: *Stepping up to plan and create activities without adult guidance, encouraging kids to unleash their own ideas and skills.*

Self-Discipline: *Managing behavior and responsibility on their own, without constant supervision, to build independence and maturity.*

Teamwork and Collaboration: *Working together as a group of diverse participants to discuss, plan, and organize camp events effectively.*

Goal-Setting and Planning: *Creating clear objectives, steps, and schedules for activities, from morning routines to fun events, to achieve a successful day.*

Adaptability to New Experiences: *Embracing unfamiliar settings and people, like a new campus or friends from other schools, to make the most of adventures like camp.*

17. In the Camp: Planning a Day

Under the soft glow of the moon hanging high in the clear night sky, the camp kids gathered in the well-lit courtyard of the school. Tall trees whispered gently in the cool breeze, their leaves sparkling like tiny stars under the moonlight. Fireflies danced around the flower beds, adding a magical twinkle to the air. The courtyard felt peaceful and alive, with the sweet scent of night-blooming jasmine floating everywhere. It was the perfect spot for friends to share ideas and dream big.

Before diving into their task, the kids started with a fun getting-to-know-each-other activity. They sat in a big circle on the soft sand, and each one shared something simple about themselves. "Hello, I'm Ravi from Town High School, Thrissur and I love drawing animals!" one boy said with a shy smile. "That's so cool! I like drawing too," someone replied kindly. "Hi, everyone! My name is Sara, I'm from the Government Girls High School, Thiruvananthapuram and my favorite game is Volleyball," a girl added, waving to the group. They went around the circle, laughing and clapping for each other. This helped everyone feel like old friends right away, with warm hellos and friendly chats filling the air.

After the activity and chatting for a few more minutes, the kids began discussing their task with friends from their own schools, then with new faces from other places. "Hey, what do you think we should do first in the morning?" one boy asked his neighbor with a big smile. "I love your idea about waking up early—let's make it fun!" a girl replied, giggling. As they talked happily, four natural groups formed, each buzzing with excitement like little beehives under the moon.

While joining one group's lively talk, Murali noticed everyone was trying to plan the whole morning at once. "Friends, this is getting a bit mixed up," he said kindly. "What if we create a big-picture plan together first? Then we can break into our four groups to handle the details. After that, we share everything in a large meeting to make it perfect. Does that sound good?"

He stepped onto a small stone platform in the courtyard and asked for attention. "Hello, dear friends! May I have two minutes to share an idea?"

Everyone looked up from their spots in the soft sand filled courtyard. "Sure, Murali! Go ahead!" a few kids called out warmly.

"Thank you so much! I suggest we first make a rough plan for tomorrow morning as one big team. Then, we split our four groups, with each one taking care of one or more parts in detail. What do you think? Could that work for us?"

"Give us an example of your rough plan," someone called out with a friendly wave.

"Okay! For instance, we could aim to challenge ourselves starting from wake-up time—to build our stamina. Other goals could be improving observation and creative thinking. We might get up extra early, get ready, help with cooking and other camp chores, do an energizing morning activity, then mix outdoor and indoor fun for the rest of the morning. We'd also leave some time for guests. That's one idea from me. What about you all? Let's hear your thoughts!"

"That covers a lot, Murali! I like how it includes everyone," Lyla said with a grin. Murali gave her a thumbs-up and said, "Thanks, Lyla! You're right—teamwork makes it better."

"Sounds good to start," most kids agreed, nodding and smiling at each other.

"Let's use our four groups," a boy shouted from the back with excitement. "One for wake-up and getting ready, one for chores and cooking, one for the energizing activity, and one for indoor and outdoor fun. Our goals: build endurance, observation, and creativity." Everyone clapped and said, "Yes! Great idea!" They chatted more, sharing laughs like, "I can't wait to help with cooking—maybe we can make funny shapes with the food!"

They quickly settled into their four groups without any fuss, sitting in cozy circles on the soft sand. Each group picked their parts and started planning with friendly talks. "What if we add a quick game to wake-up time?" one kid suggested. "Oh, yes! That would make it so much fun," another replied, high-fiving.

As they wrapped up sharing in the big group under the moonlit sky, Teacher Indira came back and sat quietly on a bench nearby, listening with a smile. They discussed each sub-plan, combined them into a single schedule, and assigned each group to execute its part. "This is coming together nicely," Murali said to the others. "Thanks to all your wonderful ideas!" They chose Helen, from one of the other schools, to present to the Teacher.

Helen explained how they organized the talks and shared the complete morning plan. "We had so much fun planning in our groups," she added with a warm smile. Each group answered the Teacher's questions kindly and made a few tweaks. Finally, Teacher Indira said, "Kids, this is a fantastic plan! We'll go with it. Thank you all so much for your great work." Then, with a kind twinkle in her eye, she added, "You know, I avoided the self-introduction session at the beginning of the camp on purpose. I wanted to see how you would organize getting to know each other yourselves—and you did it so well! Now, let's eat dinner."

After dinner, they had lots to prepare for the next day. "Hey, let's ask those helpful adults for tips—they're always so nice," one kid suggested. They even asked three helpful adults from the Teacher's team for advice, chatting and laughing as they got ready. Everyone went to bed late, after finishing all the setup, feeling happy and excited.

But Murali's mind wandered like a lost kite. He pictured his cozy room back home, with its posters of cricket stars and the shelf of adventure books he had read a hundred times. He pulled the thin blanket up to his chin and stared at the ceiling, where shadows danced like playful monkeys in the moonlight.

That was when the feeling of missing home crept in—soft as a summer breeze, yet heavy as a raincloud. Then thoughts of his little sister Hridya filled his mind. She was his shadow, his sidekick, the one who begged for piggyback rides and hid his pencils and books as "treasure" under her bed. Had she fallen asleep by now? He looked outside. The stars winked down like a thousand tiny eyes, and in their glow, he imagined Hridya gazing at the same sky from her bedroom window.

"She's okay," he whispered to the night. "And so am I." He reached into his backpack and pulled out a crumpled drawing she had slipped into his pocket that morning—a stick-figure Murali with a superhero cape.

As sleep finally tiptoed in, Murali drifted off with dreams of home woven into the wild magic of the camp. Little did he know, the real adventure was just beginning—one that would teach him that missing someone does not pull you apart; it stitches your heart even stronger.

***

Life-Skills Introduced in This Chapter

Group Organization: Forming teams naturally and dividing tasks fairly to make planning efficient and inclusive.

Idea Sharing and Leadership: Stepping up to suggest better ways, like creating a big-picture plan first, and encouraging others to join in.

Goal-Setting: Defining clear aims, such as building endurance, observation, and creativity, to guide activities and decisions.

Collaboration and Feedback: Discussing sub-plans in small groups, then combining them in a big meeting, while listening to input and making changes.

Presentation Skills: Selecting someone to clearly convey the group's ideas to adults and answering questions confidently to finalize plans.

18. In the Camp: The Finders and Fixers

The sun was still hiding when the first bell tinkled across the dormitory. “Four o’clock, little explorers!” announced the activity team. Soon, blankets flew like magic carpets, and forty sleepy smiles lit the dark. Even though they had gone to bed late, the children rose easily. The helpers were ready too. The day began with yoga at 5 a.m., led by Daya—a student who had trained as a yoga instructor—as planned by the teachers. Daya raised her hands and said in a solemn voice, “Breathe in this awesome morning, my dear friends.” An energizing 40-minute session followed, leaving everyone feeling strong and awake. At 6 a.m., they enjoyed hot morning tea.

The food team had already planned breakfast and lunch menus with the cooks the night before. They helped out during their free moments between activities.

After tea, it was time for the outdoor adventure: "Knowing the Place." This was a fun walk to explore the area around the school, set in a quiet, town-like spot. The children were divided into six teams, each with a guide from the camp staff. Six colorful maps, created with the help of local community members, rolled like treasure scrolls. The goal was clear: each child had to identify at least two special things about the places they visited, two things that needed improvement, and two ideas to make them better.

They set off with lots of energy and sang, “We are the finders, we are the fixers!” Those lines had been created during the previous night’s planning session.

As the teams walked along winding paths, the morning world came alive around them. A gentle breeze whispered through tall green trees, carrying the sweet scent of wild flowers blooming in soft pink and yellow clusters.

Dewdrops sparkled like tiny jewels on the grass, and birds chirped happily from branch to branch, as if welcoming the young explorers. The sun peeked over the hills, painting the sky in warm golden light and warming the cool earth under their feet.

Everyone, even the local children, loved discovering new spots! They found homes of people they knew, places of worship, offices, shops, markets, and small businesses. They had never realized their area was so vast, diverse, and beautiful. The paths, streets, and sidewalks offered fresh sights at every turn.

Meera found a library whose windows frowned with cracked glass. A replacement was essential. Little Priya waved at Uncle Kunjappan's tea shop and wrote, "Special: Smells like cardamom heaven." Manu noted a wobbly bench in the front yard of the Municipal Library. His ideas for improvement were to add more benches and paint them sky-blue, provide shade, and plant flowers nearby to encourage open-air reading!

Another team observed that people were using motor cars and bikes even for short distances. This was not good for the health of the environment or the people. Hence, the Municipal Council should develop campaign plans to promote walking and cycling. Yet another team's observation was connected to that. People reported that traffic was increasing day by day on municipal roads, but there were not enough walkways and cycling tracks. If walkways and cycling tracks were built, it would improve the health of the people as well as the beauty of the entire municipal area. The team that visited the hilly area demanded a hiking track and periodic trimming of bushes.

By 8 a.m., they were back, quickly bathed, and had breakfast—all on schedule. They were learning how to do things fast and efficiently.

At 9 a.m., everyone gathered in the meeting hall for sharing their observations and ideas. The Municipal Chairperson and two Municipal Councillors had also joined them. The children discussed their findings and suggested improvements. It was eye-opening for the adults! The Municipal Chairperson and Councillors said they received feedback daily, but rarely such deep thoughts and clever suggestions as those shared by the students. The Chairperson promised to use many of the ideas in planning for their municipality.

***

Life-Skills Introduced in This Chapter

Planning Skills: Turning careful observations into clear, useful ideas—such as adding benches, painting them sky-blue, planting flowers, or building walking tracks—shows how to plan real improvements step by step.

Creative Thinking: Making up a cheerful team song ("We are the finders, we are the fixers!") the night before proves that new ideas can come from fun group planning.

Map-Reading Skills: Using colorful hand-drawn maps to find homes, shops, and hidden paths teaches how to follow and understand directions on paper.

Note-Taking Skills: Writing short, clear notes like "Smells like cardamom heaven" or "wobbly bench" helps remember important details to share later.

Environmental Care: Noticing too many cars on short trips and suggesting walking or cycling paths shows how to protect nature and stay healthy.

Respect and care for Local People: Working with community members to draw spatial maps, visit their places and gathering information from them increase respect and care for local people.

Safety Awareness: Spotting cracked windows, wobbly benches, and overgrown bushes teaches children to look for things that could be unsafe and think of fixes.

Presentation Skills: Speaking clearly to the Municipal Chairperson and Councillors about findings helps children share ideas with grown-ups confidently.

Listening Skills: Hearing daily feedback is common, but truly listening to children's fresh ideas surprised the adults and taught everyone the value of every voice.

Time-Keeping Discipline: Waking at 4 a.m., finishing yoga, tea, walk, bath, and breakfast by 9 a.m. trains children to follow a tight timetable without rushing quality.

19. My Story

The next morning at camp, the activity was called "My Story." It took place outdoors, under a big old shade tree in the school yard. The children made a bright crown from cardboard and shiny paper. They wrote "My Story" on the front in sparkling glitter. They placed the crown on a small table near the tree.

Everyone sat in a neat semicircle on the ground. Teacher Indira sat on a chair facing them. She was the host. She explained the rules gently. "Anyone who wishes may volunteer. Wear the crown and share a happy moment from your life. Tell us what lesson it taught you."

To Murali's surprise, Lyla stood up first! The children clapped loudly. Even Teacher Indira joined in. Lyla gave a shy smile, put on the crown, and began in a soft voice. Soon her words grew clearer and stronger.

"Dear Teacher and friends," she said, "I never thought I would join a camp or speak in front of so many people. First, thank you, Murali, for asking me to come." More happy claps filled the air.

"You all know I am usually quiet," Lyla continued. "I do not speak much. But today feels special." Everyone smiled and clapped again.

"My voice is soft, so people sometimes do not listen carefully. This makes me lose courage, and I stay silent. One day, my family and I went boating on a lake. After some time, I noticed water seeping in through a small crack in the boat. I pointed it out to my cousin. He told the boatman. The boatman smiled and said, 'It is normal. Do not worry.' Everyone relaxed and enjoyed the ride. But I kept watching the crack. I felt it would not hold much longer.

I tried to tell others, but they only laughed and said it was fine. At last, I gathered all my courage. I stood up and shouted, 'Please listen to me!' My voice was louder than ever before. It surprised even me! The boat became quiet. 'Take us back to the shore right now!' I told the boatman. Some tried to calm me, but I did not sit down. Finally, the boatman turned the boat around.

Just as we reached the dock, there was a loud crack! A piece of the boat's floor broke. Water shot up like a fountain. Everyone shouted as the boat started to sink. Luckily, the water was shallow. We all stepped out safely and walked to the shore.

Friends, when I remember that day, three lessons shine clearly. I hope they help you too."

"Go on, Lyla!" the Teacher and children called.

"First, if I had not found the courage to speak, something scary might have happened. So, always share important thoughts bravely—it can save the day. Second, listen carefully to even the softest voices; they may carry big news. Third, be kind to everyone. Watch for the moment someone wants to speak. Give them a chance. If we are not paying attention, we might miss something precious.

Thank you for listening so patiently," Lyla ended.

Teacher Indira stood up and gave her a warm hug. She praised Lyla with shining eyes. Lyla's story touched every heart. Soon, more than ten other children took turns. Each wore the crown and shared their own special tales.

All the morning activities went smoothly and joyfully. It was a fresh, exciting experience for everyone!

***

Life Skills Introduced in This Chapter

Building Courage to Speak Up: *Finding bravery to share important thoughts or warnings, even when afraid, to prevent trouble and help others.*

Active Listening to Quiet Voices: *Paying close attention to shy or soft-spoken friends so their ideas are heard and nothing valuable is missed.*

Empathy and Consideration: *Noticing when someone wants to speak, giving them space, and showing kindness to build better understanding.*

Sharing Personal Stories: *Volunteering to tell real-life experiences in a group to inspire others, grow confidence, and create closer bonds.*

Overcoming Shyness: *Stepping outside comfort zones—joining new activities or speaking in public—with gentle encouragement from friends.*

20. In the Camp: The Sunset Planning Party

As the sun sank low, brushing the sky with warm strokes of orange and pink, it was exactly 7 o'clock on the last magical evening of summer camp. The children gathered in a tight circle, buzzing with excitement for their final planning meeting. Laughter bubbled up as they dreamed big about tomorrow's grand goodbye adventure!

Murali spoke up wisely: "Let's plan the morning of our fourth day as one big group. No teams this time. We'll see how much more organized we've become after these three wonderful days."

"Agreed!" came the cheerful chorus from everyone.

"Let's build a huge obstacle course!" Maya called out. "And a friendship chain relay race!" added another, eyes wide with sparkle. Holding hands like a band of brave explorers, they shaped and sharpened their ideas until the plan glowed brilliantly. Their teamwork turned everything golden. High-fives cracked like fireworks, and every heart swelled with the power to do anything together!

Then Lyla chimed in: "We should collect everyone's leaving times for tomorrow. It's key to making our day perfect."

"Spot on!" Nadiya agreed, and the group burst into applause.

"May I take charge of that?" Nadiya offered.

"Absolutely—go for it!" they replied. One by one, the children shared their travel plans, and Nadiya neatly entered them into a spreadsheet on the camp laptop. She added her own last and sorted the list from earliest to latest. The circle grew quiet, after a few minutes Nadiya announced: "Twenty-seven friends leave by 11 a.m., and the other twenty-three head out between 12:30 p.m. and 2:45 p.m."

"What a smart split!" said Shyam, who had quickly become the camp's star chef in just three days.

"How is it smart?" wondered Manjusha.

"Easy," Shyam explained with a grin. "The early birds get a hearty breakfast. The later group enjoys breakfast and lunch. If the teachers say yes, we could even serve breakfast and lunch to the parents who come to pick them up!"

Thunderous claps filled the air as the idea won every vote.

Now came the fun part: brainstorming ways to say a sparkling goodbye to their friends and families. "What if we make personalized friendship bracelets?" suggested Ravi, twisting his fingers like he was weaving magic. "We could hand them out with a quick note saying what we love about each person!"

"Ooh, yes! And let's line up for a 'gratitude tunnel'!" added Sofia, jumping to her feet. "Everyone stands in two rows, and as each friend walks through, we shower them with kind words—like 'You're the best storyteller!' or 'Thanks for making me laugh!' It'll feel like a wave of hugs!"

"Don't forget photo booth moments!" piped up Jamal. "Snap a picture with every group, so no one leaves without a smile frozen in time!"

"And a group cheer chant!" exclaimed Priya. "We all shout special nicknames, like 'Super Shyam the Soup Wizard!' to send them off with giggles echoing in their ears."

The ideas flowed like a river of rainbows, each one building on the last, until their farewell plan felt like the warmest, most memorable send-off ever.

Then they rushed to share it all with Teacher Indira. Her bright nod of yes sent them leaping and whooping with joy. "We're the greatest squad in the universe!" they hollered, dashing to dinner with full hearts and empty plates soon to be filled with tasty camp favorites.

***

Life Skills Introduced in This Chapter

Team work: *Learn to work in teams by matching individual priorities with the thoughts of others.*

Leadership: *Readiness and skill to lead people whenever there is a need for it.*

Reflection and Feedback: *Looking back at the day to celebrate wins and learn from them, so you grow stronger with every step.*

Planning and Problem-Solving: *Chopping big ideas into small actions, team-brainstorming fixes, and organizing like pros to reach your goals.*

Appreciation and Gratitude: *Saying "th ank you" from the heart to build sunny friendships and a thankful spirit.*

Sharing Responsibilities: *Splitting tasks fairly and chatting clearly so everyone pulls together smoothly.*

Celebrating Talents: *Spotting and sharing hidden gifts, like a beautiful voice, to boost bravery and spark creative joy!*

21. In the Camp: The Final Talent Bolster

The children felt a deep wave of happiness and pride after their grand camp plan for the departing day was approved, followed by a wonderful supper on their last evening together. But the magic of the night was far from over. Right after the tasty meal, the "Evening Recall and Arts Feast" began, filling the air with warmth and excitement!

First came the recall time. Under the sparkling stars, the friends gathered close, like a family, to share their favorite memories from the entire camp. These moments felt like a treasure chest of shining jewels in their hearts.

"Working together made every day an adventure!" one child said with a bright smile, holding a friend's hand tightly. "I learned to be brave, kind, and helpful," another added, their voice full of joy and a little tremble of emotion. They talked about the wonderful lessons they had discovered throughout the camp, like turning dreams into real successes and planning activities that brought everyone joy. The scouting activity was another unforgettable experience. They became little explorers. They walked through the locality, talked to people, and learned about real needs—like need for safer walkways and cycle tracks, clean water spots, safe play areas, maintain public assets properly, making great use of abandoned bushy areas or helping hands for elders. This opened their eyes and hearts to understand their community better, making them feel like true heroes who could make a difference.

Planning and leading their own activities felt like having a superpower. Their eyes shone with pride as they clapped and jumped, their hearts bursting with achievement!

With grateful hearts, they turned to Teacher Indira, who felt like the kindest, wisest aunt in the world. "Thank you for believing in us!" they all said together, rushing into a big group hug. This made Teacher Indira's eyes fill with happy tears, and everyone felt a special warmth that brought them even closer.

Teacher Indira smiled like a glowing lantern in the night. Her voice was soft and comforting, like a warm blanket on a cool evening. "My dear stars, you planned like true heroes! Heroes see a challenge, think of smart ideas, and move forward with courage and heart. You created a big plan, broke it into fun steps, formed teams with cheers and help, listened to good advice, and finished with great success. You shared tasks fairly, so everyone could shine. That is why your camp was such a triumph! Hold this close forever and sprinkle it on your lives—you're all bound for bright, wonderful futures!"

Suddenly, the signature music of the final day Arts Feast, which they found the music teacher was composing the previous day, began to play in the auditorium! Teacher Indira, with a playful twinkle in her eye, surprised them by discovering various hidden gifts among the children—singing, dancing, storytelling, and even funny skits. Before their previously planned group items, she invited them one by one to perform, and to everyone's delight, even the children themselves gasped and laughed in amazement! "How did you know I could do this?" they asked, cheeks pink with excited flutters.

"I've watched you closely all camp," she said with a grin, "and my helpful team noticed your special sparks!"

"Who is on this amazing team?" the children asked eagerly, linking arms in a circle of wonder. Their friendships felt stronger than ever, like a glowing campfire.

Teacher Indira laughed warmly and pulled them all into another hug, making them feel like one big, loving family. "I could not create this magic alone, my dears! It is a team of wonderful helpers—teachers from every school, caring parents, and kind friends from the community. They have supported us all along, and more will join tomorrow, just like our local leaders did today!" The children clapped loudly, their applause full of love for this big circle of care. It made the camp feel like the safest, happiest home. Teacher Indira's kindness touched their hearts deeply, making their bond feel unbreakable and forever.

That special night, the children performed amazingly—songs soared like colorful birds, dances swirled with grace, stories brought laughter and tears of joy, and skits sparkled with fun. They even took requests from their friends. "Tell the adventure tale!" one called out. "Or dance to the friendship song!" another begged with a big smile. Laughter echoed everywhere and hands clapped in rhythm. Their connections grew into precious, lasting treasures. It was a joyful, heart-filled ending that stayed in their souls forever—the perfect close to the best camp adventure!

***

Life-Skills Introduced in This Chapter

Reflection and Feedback: *Thinking back on the camp's events to see what went well, what was learned, and how to grow from experiences.*

Planning and Problem-Solving: *Breaking down big tasks into clear steps, brainstorming ideas, and working as a team to reach goals successfully.*

Appreciation and Gratitude: *Saying thank you to others for their help and belief, building strong relationships, and developing a thankful heart.*

Celebrating Talents: *Discovering and sharing hidden skills, like singing, dancing, and storytelling, to build confidence and enjoy creative fun together.*

Community building: *Learn how to build strong and stable societies.*

22. In the Camp: An Everlasting Goodbye Day

The sun rose with a golden smile on the fourth and final day of the summer camp. The children woke early, their hearts filled with joy and a touch of sadness.

As soon as the morning bell rang, all the friends gathered in one large circle. There were no teams today—only one big, happy family. They were ready to bring to life the careful plan they had made the night before. The giant obstacle course began as they had imagined. Children crawled under low ropes, leapt over soft mats, and balanced on narrow wooden beams. Laughter echoed as they cheered one another. "You can do it!" they called, reaching out hands to steady friends who swayed. Teachers gave them cute presents when they reached the other side.

Next came the friendship chain relay race. Everyone linked arms in a long, winding line. They passed a bright red ball from the first child to the last, racing against an imaginary clock. When the ball reached the end, the whole chain jumped with delight. Their teamwork made them swift and strong.

While the games continued, Nadiya opened her neat list on the camp laptop. Twenty-seven friends would leave by eleven o'clock. The remaining twenty-three would depart between half-past twelve and a quarter to three. This clear plan guided the cooks perfectly.

In the kitchen, Shyam the star chef smiled widely. The early leavers enjoyed a hearty breakfast of warm pancakes and juicy fruit. The later group ate both breakfast and a tasty lunch. Parents arriving to collect their children were warmly invited to share the meals. Plates clinked softly, and every face glowed with welcome.

As the morning slipped by, the children turned to their sparkling farewell ideas. Ravi and his helpers sat at a sunny table covered with colorful strings and shiny beads. They wove personalized friendship bracelets for every camper. With each careful knot, they whispered kind words. “This blue bead is for your brave heart,” Ravi told one friend. A tiny note was tied to each bracelet: “I love your funny jokes!” or “You are the best listener!”

Soon it was time for the gratitude tunnel. The children formed two long lines facing each other. As the first group of early leavers walked slowly through, gentle words rained down like soft petals. “You’re the best storyteller!” called Sofia. “Thank you for sharing your toys!” shouted Jamal. Smiles shone brightly, and a few friends brushed away happy tears.

Jamal set up the photo booth next. Bright props—silly hats, oversized sunglasses, and cardboard stars—waited in a cheerful pile. Groups of friends posed together. Snap! The camera captured goofy faces and warm hugs. Each picture became a precious keepsake.

Near the camp gate, Priya led the group cheer chant. Whenever a car arrived, everyone shouted special nicknames. “Super Shyam the Soup Wizard!” they cheered for the chef. “Amazing Maya the Idea Maker!” they called for another. Laughter filled the air, and departing friends waved until they vanished from sight.

Teacher Indira watched with shining eyes. Parents, teachers, and kind community friends lent helping hands. The camp felt like one large, loving family. Every child left with a bracelet on their wrist, a photo in their pocket, joy in their heart and learning for the entire life.

When the last car rolled away, the remaining three children—Murali and his two close neighbours—gathered for a quiet moment. They lived nearby and would soon cycle home together. The campers had turned their plan into a day of pure magic! Friendships had grown deeper, and memories sparkled like stars. The grand goodbye was complete—simple, kind, and full of love.

***

Life Skills Introduced in this Chapter

Teamwork and Cooperation: *Working together as one big group to complete games and activities.*

Planning and Organization: *Using a clear schedule to manage meals and goodbyes for different leaving times.*

Gratitude and Kindness: *Sharing sincere compliments and thank-yous through words, notes, and bracelets.*

Creativity and Celebration: *Making bracelets, taking photos, and cheering with nicknames to honor friendships.*

Inclusion and Care: *Welcoming parents and ensuring every child felt loved and remembered.*

23. Back at Sweet Home

Murali pedalled his bicycle steadily along the familiar road, his legs tired but his spirit soaring. He felt like a brave knight returning from a grand adventure, eager to share his tales with those he loved most.

He recollected how Hridya's small heart had ached when he waved goodbye last Friday evening! She missed her big brother terribly—she would not see his cheerful smiles for three long days. Tears filled her eyes as she held tightly to his bag. "Please don't go, Brother!" she pleaded, her voice trembling like a leaf in the wind. Mother drew her into a gentle hug and whispered, "Darling, the time will pass quickly, like a bird. Soon, he will return with wonderful stories."

Yet, on Tuesday morning, Hridya sprang from bed as the first light touched the window. Her eyes shone with excitement. "It is holiday time—did you forget?" Mother said with a soft laugh. Hridya shook her head firmly. "No, Mom! Brother is coming home today!" Butterflies danced in her stomach as she dressed in a hurry, ate her breakfast swiftly, and took her place in the front yard like a watchful guard. Father, Mother, Grandfather, and Grandmother smiled warmly. "Be patient, little one," they said. "He will arrive only in the afternoon." But Hridya paid no heed; her mind was filled with dreams of her brother. She stared down the road, her heart beating like a happy drum. She counted each minute, picturing the warm hugs and exciting stories ahead. By eleven o'clock, Mother and Father had to leave for school to help with new admissions. They departed with bright smiles, whispering to each other, "The love between our children is the greatest gift."

Her grandparents had to force her a lot to eat lunch.

At precisely 3:15 p.m, a merry bicycle bell rang at the gate—the most joyful sound Hridya had ever heard! Her heart jumped with delight. "Brother is here! He is truly here!" she shouted to Grandfather and Grandmother, dashing to open the gate with flying feet. Grandfather followed quickly, smiling broadly. From the windowsill, their soft kitten Charu, with her glossy black-and-white fur, saw the commotion. She let out a joyful meow, jumped down gracefully, and raced ahead like a speedy arrow.

Murali leaped from his bike, his face glowing like the morning sun. He knelt down, and Hridya rushed into his arms for the warmest, strongest hug imaginable. She held him close, as if to keep him forever. Happy tears sparkled in her eyes. Hridya kissed his cheeks with big, wet smacks—mwah! Mwah!—and her questions poured out like a rushing stream. "Tell me all about it, Brother! Who joined the camp? What delicious foods did you eat? What exciting games did you play? Did the teachers teach serious lessons, or was it full of laughter and fun?" Her words came so fast that no one else could speak. Charu climbed onto his shoulder, purring softly like a gentle motor, her tail waving happily.

Grandmother chuckled kindly, her eyes moist with happiness at the loving scene. "Allow your brother to enter the house first, my dear princess!" But Murali was thrilled to be home, surrounded by his sister's affection. With a kind smile, he answered every question patiently. He described the camp in vivid detail—the tall trees, the sparkling river, the friends he made, and the games under the stars. Hridya listened with wide eyes, imagining every moment as if she were there.

As the afternoon sun warmed the yard, the family gathered on the veranda for a simple meal. Grandfather brought cool lemonade, and Grandmother served fresh fruits from the garden. Murali told more stories: how they built a campfire and sang songs, how they learned to tie strong knots, and how a friendly peacock visited one evening. Hridya clapped her hands in wonder. "I want to see a peacock too!" she exclaimed. Charu curled up in Murali's lap, content and purring.

Soon, Mother and Father returned from school. They hugged Murali tightly, their faces full of pride. "Welcome home, our adventurer," Father said. Mother added, "We are so glad you are safe and happy." The whole family sat together, sharing laughter and snacks. Hridya held Murali's hand, not wanting to let go.

Finally, as the sky turned golden with sunset, Hridya looked up at her brother with shining eyes. "Brother, when I go to camp someday, you must come with me. Promise?"

Murali's heart filled with warmth. He ruffled her hair gently and replied, "We shall plan many adventures together, my little explorer." Hand in hand, they walked inside, with Charu trotting beside them. Murali stroked her soft fur, feeling the cozy embrace of home in every heartbeat. What a joyful, loving end to the most wonderful camp!

***

Life-Skills Introduced in This Chapter

Patience and Listening: *Waiting calmly for loved ones and listening carefully to their stories, even when eager, to build stronger family ties.*

Expressing Emotions: *Sharing feelings of sadness when saying goodbye or joy upon reunion, to create open and trusting relationships.*

Curiosity and Asking Questions: *Asking thoughtful questions about others' experiences to learn new things and show interest in their lives.*

Family Support and Affection: *Greeting family members with hugs, kisses, and kind words to express love and make everyone feel valued.*

Caring for Pets: *Including pets in family activities, petting them gently, and noticing their happiness to practice kindness and responsibility.*

About the Author

P. Anil Prasad (sometimes credited as Anil Prasad P) is a retired government servant, educator, writer, and lifelong advocate for open knowledge from India.

He began teaching at fifteen, tutoring young children. Later, he was trained and certified as a Primary School Teacher and worked briefly at a charitable school. While pursuing his undergraduate degree in English Language and Literature through distance education—and afterward—he and a few friends organized skill training and welfare activities for school students, funded by tutoring in private institutions.

At twenty-eight, he joined the Government of Kerala's Finance Department, serving in key roles: Assistant Programme Officer (Modernizing Government Programme), Nodal Officer – Training, deputed Director – Lifelong Learning for the Additional Skill Acquisition Programme (ASAP) under the Higher Education Department, Additional Secretary in Finance, and Secretary to the 7th State Finance Commission.

A passionate training facilitator, Anil has designed and delivered hundreds of learning programmes on diverse topics. His deep commitment to open education led him to conduct international workshops for the Commonwealth of Learning (COL), Canada, and contribute to WikiEducator.

He publishes most of his works—spanning short stories, novels, poetry, philosophy, and educational literature in English and Malayalam—under Creative Commons (CC-BY-SA) licences to keep knowledge free and accessible.

Anil lives in Thiruvananthapuram, Kerala, with his wife (a school teacher) and daughter (an Electronics & Instrumentation engineer).

Select Published Works

(All works except where noted are released under CC-BY-SA open licence)

1. The Netizens (Short Stories), 2012 – ISBN: 978-1477682609
2. The Quake and Other Stories, 2012 – ISBN: 978-1478376873

3. Bhukambavum Mattu Kathakalum (Malayalam Short Stories), 2012 – ISBN: 978-1479268764
4. Athirukalillathe Arivinte Lokam (Malayalam, on Internet & learning), 2012 – ISBN: 978-1479268764
5. Cardinal Rules for a Calm and Pleasant Life (Philosophy), 2014 – ISBN: 978-1500556259

6–8. Imanofutu trilogy (Science Fiction), 2013–2015
   - Vol. 1: A 21st-Century Portrait – ISBN: 978-1478341864
   - Vol. 2: The Eventful Start of Sugirl's Presidency – ISBN: 978-1505514445
   - Vol. 3: The First Alien Home on Earth – ISBN: 978-1511583053

9. Neither She Nor He; It's Me (Novel), 2015 – ISBN: 978-1516994380
10. Mazhayile Kathakal (Malayalam Short Stories), Prabhath Book House
11. Let Me Seek It (Anthology), Kindle, 2020 – ASIN: B083JKPLXY
12. "Management of Lifelong Learning: From Individuals to Learning Organisations and Societies" (co-authored paper), PCF10, Commonwealth of Learning, September 2022

Connect

Email: apletters@zohomail.in
Website / blog: www.apletters.in
X / LinkedIn / Zoho / Arattai: @apletters

www.ingramcontent.com/pod-product-compliance
Lightning Source LLC
Chambersburg PA
CBHW050021170726
48282CB00025B/493
* 9 7 8 9 3 5 5 9 2 3 4 3 1 *